Mighty mo

by Alison Brown

tiger tales

Mo was bored.

Bored, bored, bored.

"There must be SOMETHING amazing I can do," Mo said.

Hettie was making
incredible ice creams.
"That's IT!" cried Mo.
"I can do that!"

"Triple scoop, coming up!"

sNAp!

Albert was incredible with balloons.

"I can do **THAT.** They'll call me

MAGNIFICENT *Mo* — **POWer-puffer!"**

"Oops!"

"Oh, No, No, No!
Too MUCH
Puff!"

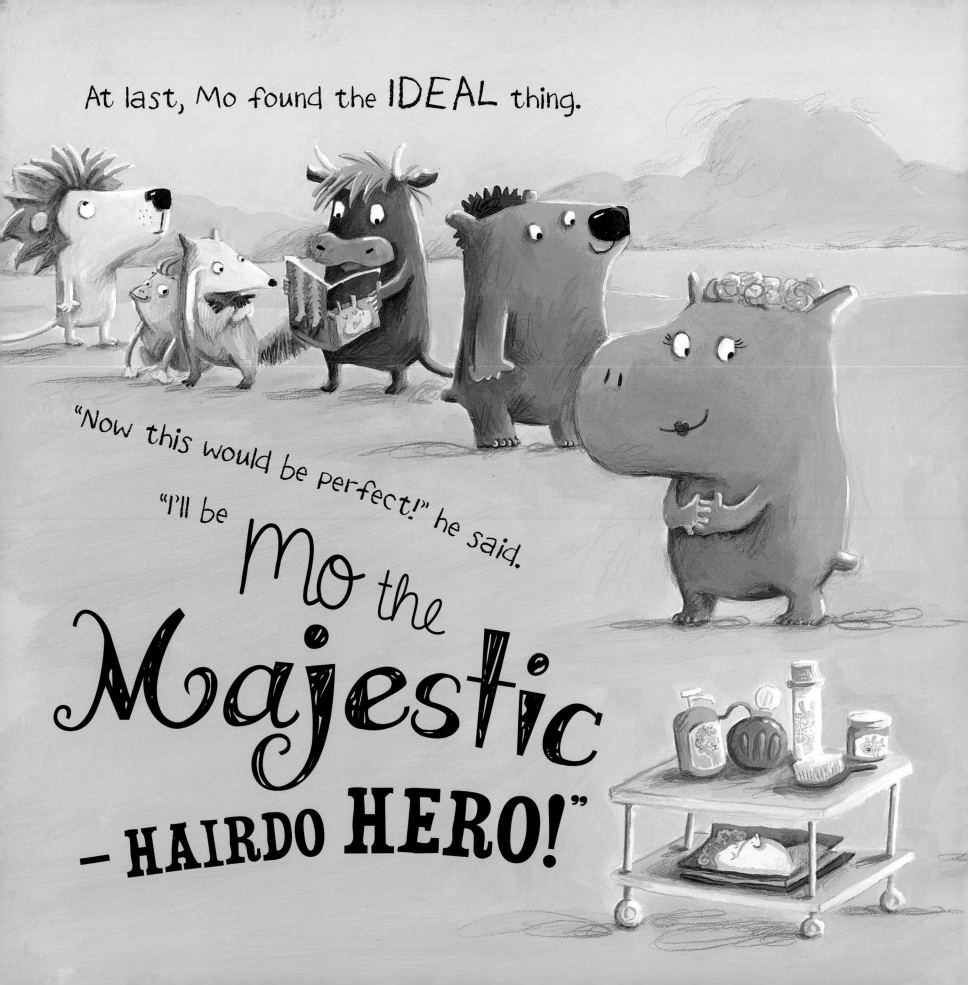

"I'm not coming out again. EVER!"

"Don't give up, Mo," said his friends. "You'll find SOMETHING SPECIAL to do!"

Just at that moment they heard a commotion . . . .

"HELP! HELP!"

"What's the panic, Percy?" asked Mo.
"Big Ron has stolen the Golden Dodo!"
Percy squeaked. "We need YOU, Mo!"

"ME? Why me?"

"You're **super-strong!** You're **super-fast!**" cried Percy. "Only YOU can catch Big Ron!"

"Fantastic!" said Mo. "At last! Something amazing I can do!"

OTCHA!"

"Put me down!"
Big Ron yelled.

And so Mo did
just that . . .